For Gwen Sherwood and
her grandson, Ryan.
– G.S.

For my daughters,
Ema and Mima!
– P.L.

First published 2011 by Macmillan Children's Books
a division of Macmillan Publishers Limited
20 New Wharf Road, London N1 9RR
Basingstoke and Oxford
Associated companies throughout the world
www.panmacmillan.com

ISBN: 978-0-230-75444-7 (HB)
ISBN: 978-0-230-75445-4 (PB)

Text copyright © Gillian Shields 2011
Illustrations copyright © Polona Lovšin 2011
Moral rights asserted.

1 3 5 7 9 8 6 4 2

A CIP catalogue for this book is available from the British Library.
Printed in China

The Littlest Bear

Written by
Gillian Shields

Illustrated by
Polona Lovšin

MACMILLAN CHILDREN'S BOOKS

The littlest bear had soft, white fur and a smudgy black nose, and he loved to play in the snow.

"Don't go too far!" said his mother. "You're so little that the wild white wolf might catch you."

"I'm not scared of the wild white wolf!" laughed the littlest bear.
"You should be," said the mother bear. "He has huge eyes
like the sun and his teeth are as sharp as ice."

"Oooh!" said the littlest bear,
and he hid next to his mother.

Every day the littlest bear chased snowflakes,

and splashed in the water, but he was careful not to go too far.

"I wish I had someone to play with," he sighed, looking out over the cold, white land.

When the day was over, the littlest bear snuggled next to his mother. The stars shone and the wind howled over the ice.

As he was falling asleep, the littlest bear thought about the wild white wolf's yellow eyes and sharp teeth, and he was glad that his mother was near.

The littlest bear grew strong enough
to trek across the snow with his mother,
stepping into her big paw prints.

Sometimes he noticed the prints of other creatures.
"Do they belong to another little bear?" he asked.
"That would be fun!"

But his mother said, "Stay next to me.
Those marks are wolf tracks!"

One night, the wind blew more fiercely than ever. The
littlest bear was frightened. "Don't worry," his mother said.
"Go to sleep, little one." And she closed her eyes.

The littlest bear closed his eyes too. He lay on his front.

He lay on his back.

He covered his ears with his paws.

But even though the littlest bear tried and tried, he could not go to sleep.

All night long, the wind sang and the stars blazed. The littlest bear saw strange and beautiful lights, dancing across the sky like a giant bear.

He forgot all about being frightened. He forgot about everything.

Slowly, he walked away from his sleeping
mother and gazed up at the sky.
"Oh!" said the littlest bear. "It's all so . . . big."

But when the lights faded and the sky grew dark again, the littlest bear remembered that he shouldn't have gone so far.

The wind whipped over the snow, and a voice floated on the wind. It was a voice like a howling wolf!

"Oh dear, oh help!" cried the littlest bear,
and he tried to run back to his mother.

But as he ran, he slipped on the ice
and fell, roly-poly, down a snow hill
and into . . .

. . . the littlest wolf, who was crying in the middle of the cold, white land, because he was lost.

"Oh help!" cried the littlest wolf.
"You're a wild white bear!
My mother said you would
catch me if I went too far!"

"But you're a wild white wolf!"
cried the littlest bear. "My mother
said *you* would catch *me!*"

And they both hid in the deep, soft
snow and waited to be caught.

They waited and waited, but nothing happened!
So they stopped hiding.

"You haven't got huge eyes like
the sun," said the littlest bear.

"And you haven't got enormous paws
like the moon," said the littlest wolf.

The littlest bear and the littlest wolf
looked at each other and laughed.

"Did you see the lights?" they asked eagerly.
"Can you catch snowflakes? Do you want to play?"

When the sun rose, the mother bear and the mother wolf woke up and went to look for their little ones, but they saw each other first . . .

"Wolf!" growled the mother bear.

"Bear!" snapped
the mother wolf.

The littlest bear and the littlest wolf rushed towards
their mothers, shouting, "But he's my friend!"

Slowly, slowly, the mother wolf looked
at the littlest bear . . . and smiled.

Slowly, slowly, the mother bear looked
at the littlest wolf . . . and laughed.

After that, the friends played together every day.

"Good morning, wild white bear," called the littlest wolf.

"Hello, wild white wolf," shouted the littlest bear. "Race you to the water!"

They chased snowflakes,

and did roly-polies.

They raced and tumbled and laughed,
and pretended to be big and wild and fierce.

But when the night came, the littlest
bear always went back to his mother
to snuggle next to her and fall asleep.

And if he heard a howling across the ice,
he wasn't frightened any more . . .

. . . because he knew it was just his friend,
the littlest wolf, calling out to say goodnight!